I AM READING

Friends Forever

SALLY GRINDLEY

Illustrated by

PENNY DANN

MACMILLAN CHILDREN'S BOOKS

First published by Kingfisher 2007

This edition published 2013 by Macmillan Children's Books
a division of Macmillan Publishers Limited
20 New Wharf Road, London N1 9RR
Basingstoke and Oxford
Associated companies throughout the world
www.panmacmillan.com

These stories first published by Kingfisher as
What Are Friends For? (1998) and *What Will I Do Without You?* (1999)

ISBN 978-1-4472-0966-9

Text copyright © Sally Grindley 1998, 1999, 2007
Illustrations copyright © Penny Dann 1998, 1999, 2007

The right of Sally Grindley and Penny Dann to be identified as the author and illustrator of this work
has been asserted by them in accordance with the Copyright, Designs and Patents Act 1988.

1 3 5 7 9 8 6 4 2

A CIP catalogue record for this book is available from the British Library.

Printed in China

Contents

What Are Friends For?
4

What Will I Do Without You?
23

What Are Friends For?

Jefferson Bear and Figgy Twosocks
went walking one day in the sunny
green woods.

"JB," asked Figgy Twosocks, "are you
my friend?"

"Yes," said Jefferson Bear. "I am your friend, and you are my friend."

"But what is a friend for?" asked Figgy Twosocks.

"Well . . ." said Jefferson Bear. "A friend is for playing."

"Goody," said Figgy Twosocks. "Let's play hide-and-seek."

Figgy Twosocks hid in a hollow tree.

Jefferson Bear looked everywhere, but he couldn't find her.

When it was his turn, he hid behind a tree stump. Figgy Twosocks found him straightaway.

"You're better at this than me," said Jefferson Bear.

"I'll help you this time," said Figgy Twosocks.

She hid under a pile of leaves, but left the tip of her tail showing.

The next day, Figgy Twosocks asked,
"JB, what else is a friend for?"
"Well," said Jefferson Bear, "a friend
is for sharing."

"What do *best* friends share?" asked
Figgy Twosocks.

"Well," said Jefferson Bear, "best
friends share their favourite things."

Figgy Twosocks darted off through
the woods. When she came
back, she was tugging an
enormous bramble
covered with
blackberries.

"Would you like some, JB?" she said.
"Blackberries are my favourites.
Yummy, aren't they?"
"De-licious," said
Jefferson Bear.

That afternoon, loud squeals woke
Jefferson Bear from his sleep.

Yelp! Yelp! Yelp!
Yelp! Yelp!

"I'm coming," he
bellowed. "What's
the matter?"

11

He found Figgy Twosocks lying on
the ground.

"You've got a thorn in your foot.
Keep still and I'll take it out."

"Will it hurt?" whimpered Figgy.

"I'll be as gentle as I can," said
Jefferson Bear. He closed his teeth
round the thorn and pulled.

As soon as it was out, Figgy Twosocks jumped up and pranced around.

"Thank you for helping me, JB," she said.

"That's what friends are for," said Jefferson Bear.

The next afternoon, Jefferson Bear
was dozing in the sun. Figgy Twosocks
wanted to play. She crept up behind
him and yelled . . .

"Boo!"

Jefferson Bear nearly jumped out of his wobbly fur. Figgy Twosocks ran round and round squealing, "Made you jump! Made you jump!"

Jefferson Bear didn't think it was funny.

"Go away, Figgy Twosocks," he said.

"You have made me cross."

"But I want to play," said Figgy
Twosocks.

"And I want to sleep," said Jefferson
Bear. "A big brown bear needs his sleep.
Go and play somewhere else."

"You're not my friend any more,"
said Figgy Twosocks sadly, and she
trudged off.

When Jefferson Bear woke
up the next morning,
he felt sorry he had
upset his friend.

"I'll play with her today," he said to
himself.

But Figgy Twosocks stayed away.

Jefferson Bear began to worry. He went
to her den and called, "Figgy
Twosocks, are you all right?"
There was no reply.

Jefferson Bear's worry grew.

He walked to the edge of the river

and called again, "Where are you,

Figgy Twosocks?"

But there was no reply.

Jefferson Bear's worry grew bigger.

He walked through the woods calling,

"Come out, Figgy Twosocks, it's me,

Jefferson Bear."

But there was still no reply.

At last he came to a hollow
tree where he saw the tip
of a tail sticking out.
"Figgy Twosocks, is that you?"
he called. "It's JB."
He listened and thought
he heard a sniff.

The sniff grew louder and louder until
it turned into a

GREAT BIG SOB.

"Figgy Twosocks, please come out,"
said Jefferson Bear. "I miss you."
"I'm sorry, JB," said Figgy Twosocks.
"I didn't mean
to make you
cross."

"And I'm sorry I was so grumpy," said Jefferson Bear. "Let's go and play."

"JB," sniffed Figgy Twosocks, "does that mean you're still my friend?"

"Of course I'm still your friend," said Jefferson Bear. "A friend is forever."

What Will I Do Without You?

Winter was on its way. Jefferson Bear was fat and his fur wobbled more than ever.

"Shall we go for our walk?" asked Figgy Twosocks.

"No time to walk, Figgy," said Jefferson Bear. "I'm getting ready to hibernate."

"What's hibernate?" asked Figgy.

"Hibernate is what big brown bears do in the winter," said Jefferson Bear. "It's when I go to sleep and don't wake up until spring."

"But what will I do without you?" asked Figgy.

"I'll be back before you know it," said Jefferson Bear.

The air turned frosty.

"Time for bed," yawned Jefferson Bear.

"Don't go yet," said Figgy Twosocks.

But Jefferson Bear hugged her tight
and disappeared into his cave.

"I'll miss you, JB," called Figgy.

Next morning, it was snowing.

Figgy had never seen snow before.

She ran to tell Jefferson Bear.

"JB, are you asleep yet?" she called.

A rumbly snore echoed from deep inside his cave.

Figgy kicked at the snow.

ZZZ ZZZ ZZZ!

"What good is snow when your best friend isn't there to share it?"

BIFF! BIFF! BIFF!

Figgy's brothers were
having a snowball fight.

"Can I play?" Figgy Twosocks asked.
"If you want," said Big Smudge.

"Take this," said Floppylugs.

BIFF!

"Stop it!" Figgy squealed. "That hurts."

"You wanted to play," they said and ran

off laughing.

"You wouldn't do that if

JB was here," she cried.

Then Figgy Twosocks had an idea . . .
All day long she
pushed and patted
the snow.

All day long she rolled and scooped
and shaped it.

At last, she found three black stones
and a little twig.
She stood back.

"Every time I look at my Big White
Snow Bear, I will think of JB," she said.
But Figgy Twosocks still felt very lonely.
She sobbed a great big sob.

Then she began to feel cross.

If JB was her friend, how could

he leave her for so long?

PIFF! – she threw a snowball

at the Snow Bear.

PIFF! – and another.

And another – PIFF!

"Hey, don't do that. You'll spoil it," called a voice. It was Hoptail, the squirrel. "JB's not my friend any more," said Figgy Twosocks.

"Why not?" asked Hoptail. "He's not here when I need him." "But he needs his sleep," said Hoptail. "And I need some help. I must find the nuts I buried in the autumn."

Hoptail pointed to places where she thought her food was hidden.

Figgy Twosocks dug through the snow and earth to find the nuts.

Day after day, more snow fell.

Figgy Twosocks and Hoptail ran through the woods making patterns with their pawprints.

They broke off
icicles and
watched them
melt through
their paws.

And together they
rebuilt the Big White
Snow Bear.

At the end of each day, Figgy Twosocks went to see the Big White Snow Bear. "I hope JB won't mind me having another friend," she said.

Little by little, the days grew warmer.

"The Snow Bear is melting!"

cried Figgy.

"What's happening?"

"Spring is coming,"

said Hoptail.

Suddenly, Big Smudge and Floppylugs

appeared. They clambered onto the

Snow Bear and pushed –

HEAVE . . .

WHOOSH!

The head of the
Snow Bear rolled
down the hill.

"OUCH, that hurt,"
growled a great big voice.

Big Smudge and Floppylugs
ran away.

There was Jefferson Bear, rubbing
his nose.

"That's a fine welcome back," he said.

"JB!" squealed Figgy.
"Oh, I've missed
you so much.

I built a Snow Bear to
remind me of you and
I hope you don't
mind, I've—"
"Yes?" said Jefferson Bear.
"I've made a new friend – this is
Hoptail."

Jefferson Bear laughed. "Slow down, Figgy. Let's all go for a walk and you can tell me just what you did without me."

About the Author and Illustrator

Sally Grindley is an award-winning author with many books to her name. She has written three other I Am Reading books: *The Giant Postman, Captain Pepper's Pets,* and *The Perfect Monster.*

Penny Dann has illustrated many books for children. She lives by the sea in a house with a pretty garden. When she's not drawing pictures she likes to travel around the world.

Tips for Beginner Readers

1. Think about the cover and the title of the book. What do you think it will be about? While you are reading, think about what might happen next and why.

2. As you read, ask yourself if what you're reading makes sense. If it doesn't, try rereading or look at the pictures for clues.

3. If there is a word that you do not know, look carefully at the letters, sounds, and word parts that you do know. Blend the sounds to read the word. Is this a word you know? Does it make sense in the sentence?

4. Think about the characters, where the story takes place, and the problems the characters in the story faced. What are the important ideas in the beginning, middle and end of the story?

5. Ask yourself questions like:
Did you like the story?
Why or why not?
How did the author make it fun to read?
How well did you understand it?

Maybe you can understand the story better if you read it again!